Tales from the Canyons of the Damned

Daniel Arthur Smith

Tales from the Canyons of the Damned No. 15

First Edition

Special thanks to Jessica West

ISBN-13: 978-1946777225 ISBN-10: 1946777226

Cover By Daniel Arthur Smith with original art from Lucas Marsman

Horror Fiction from Holt Smith ltd
Agroland
Tower

~*~

For Susan, Tristan, & Oliver, as all things are.

~*~

Lot 187

Jason LaVelle

~*~

A fresh bottle, Puritan Black, from Immortal Ink's *Hell Grinders* line of tattoo inks. The eight-ounce bottle was tall and smooth, with a black and silver label showing the silhouette of a puritan man with his dark black hat and black suit, only this puritan had glowing red eyes and two bony horns, giving him a clearly demonic look. It was an irony that Zane appreciated. Under the words *Puritan Black*, written in bold silver, was another line of text that read, *Lot No. 187*. Zane liked that too. There was something a little devilish about the batch of ink having the same number as the police code for murder. The *Hell Grinders* line of inks were all hand-made, giving them a unique quality. Because they weren't machine mixed, each batch of ink had a slightly different color. Even if it was infinitesimal, the serious artists like Zane felt like they could see the difference, and would never use two different lot numbers on the same piece, and sometimes not on the same person.

Wearing blue nitrile gloves, Zane cracked the seal on the bottle. There was no pressurization in the bottle of ink, so there was no spray from the top, but he always felt like he could smell the flavor of the fresh ink wafting up to him. An almost indiscernible smile settled on his face, then he sat back in his chair. He carefully inverted the bottle of ink over the top of four small plastic ink cups. He squeezed the black ink into the tiny cups, filling the first one completely, then decreasing the amount for each cup until there was less than a quarter of a cupful in the final one. He resealed his new bottle of ink, and set it above his workstation in a cabinet with a hinged glass door. He rotated it so that he could see the brand and name. He liked his inks to be organized. Not only did it soothe what he had always assumed to be a mild obsessive-compulsive disorder, it looked nice, and he wanted his clients to know that he was well put together, organized.

He stripped the gloves off and tossed them into his waste receptacle, opening the lid with the small foot pedal at the base of the bin. He wiped his hands on a paper towel, they always got sweaty inside the gloves, then donned another pair. With a disposable pipette, Zane suctioned water from a paper Dixie Cup on top of his desk and carefully added some to each of the three ink cups. He left one cup unaltered, the rest would be slightly diluted, giving him different shades of gray to work with. It was an acquired skill, mixing and diluting the ink correctly, but one he had learned well over the first fifteen years of his tattooing career. Not only did this method save tons of money by eliminating the need for bottles of different grays, it also gave his colors a more unique look, and because they were hand-mixed, they weren't easily duplicated. Zane took inventory of the equipment he had laid out on the desk in front of him. The entire work space was covered in a layer of Saran Wrap. Two tattoo machines bagged in clear plastic sandwich bags—one a coil-driven liner, the other a rotary shading machine—rested on their sides. The machines had already been loaded with disposable plastic tubes and needles appropriate for the job. His four cups of ink were ready. He peered into the Dixie Cup to ensure that there was enough rinse water for this tattoo. His bottle of green soap sat next to the machines. That too had been wrapped in Saran. His mental checklist complete, Zane finally rotated on his seat.

His client was sitting in the booth with him, silently watching as Zane completed his set-up. Her face lit up expectantly. She looked excited, but the glassiness of her eyes betrayed the bittersweet feeling she had about the tattoo.

"Let's see how this stencil is looking," Zane told her, and the woman nodded, leaning to her side a bit. She wore tight, short shorts—*booty shorts*, he called them—that showed off her legs all the way up to the very bottom of her butt cheeks. The stencil was high on the outside of her thigh, where the flesh was fairly flat and firm, excellent to work with. Zane snapped a fresh pair of gloves on and tapped at the stenciled skin.

"Perfect, it's good and dry. Are you ready, Clara?"

The woman nodded.

"Are you positive? We want to be sure. Do you want to take another look in the mirror?"

Clara looked down at her thigh, at the purple stencil depicting a boy's young face, and shook her head.

"No, it's perfect right there," she said, and this time Zane felt like she was a little more confident.

It was a large tattoo, slightly larger that Zane's palm, fingers and all, and it was detailed, as all portraits are. Zane gave her a thin smile and turned away from her. He connected his clip cord to the bright purple lining machine and tapped the foot pedal. As he did so, Zane adjusted a dial on his machine's power supply unit, changing the pitch and intensity of the machine, fine tuning it until he liked the feel and sound. Somewhere between a hum and a buzz was perfect. Zane dipped the tip of the machine into his ink, hitting the pedal to activate the machine while the needle was in the ink. This caused the machine to draw up a small amount of ink into the tube that held the needle, much like a ballpoint pen's ink reservoir. He held the machine close to a clean sheet of paper towel and ran the needle a few more times, letting a little of the excess ink spray off so that it wouldn't splatter onto his client's skin, making it more difficult for him to see his stencil. Zane turned on his stool.

"Okay Clara, here we go," he said. With one hand, he stretched the skin of her thigh, making it tauter as he leaned over her leg. He brought his machine down, and just before it touched her, Zane activated the pedal and the needle began its fast dance against her skin. For just a moment, Clara tensed. Then she relaxed as her body acclimated to the sensation. The machine thrummed, the needle plunging into her with five fine points configured in the shape of a tiny pentagram, each penetrating the skin and pushing Puritan Black beneath it.

Every few minutes Zane glanced up, checking on Clara. She was pressed back against the leather chair. Her eyes were closed but tears ran down her cheeks. He knew it wasn't from pain. Well, not the pain he was causing her anyway. It was the pain of memories, of a soul tortured. Zane dipped the needle into the ink and drew more up to begin again. His smooth, bald head once again leaned over Clara as he worked, squinting to see the finest details of her son's face. He took his time, focusing on the art, on the shadows on the boy's face, on the gentle rise at the corners of his mouth. He worked not only from the stencil, but from a photograph Clara had given him of the boy. It was the same photo they had displayed at his funeral.

Zane's hands were soggy from sweating and sore when he finally broke for lunch. Clara's tattoo was a four-hour ordeal, and it taxed him more than physically. In the beginning it hadn't been so bad, when he was creating a ghostly halo to encircle the boy's head. But once the eyes appeared, so big and filled with life, reflecting the light of a window as he looked at his mother, then it became difficult. He thought of his own son, who was nearly five years old now, no older than Clara's son had been on the day someone drove a little too close to the curb. Maybe they were distracted by their phone, or perhaps they just didn't see the boy there, splashing around in the big pile of leaves on the side of the road.

Zane shivered and lit a cigarette. He pressed his back against the outside wall of the shop, trying not to think of leaves strewn about the street, sticky with blood and pieces of Clara's son. He had known the story of Clara's son before she came in for the tattoo; it had been all over the local news three months prior, the newscasters calling it a wakeup call for motorists and parents alike.

I'm going to keep a more watchful eye on Graham, he told himself, *I'll never let something like that happen.* But even as he thought the words, he knew there were too many uncertainties in life for him to be able to constantly protect his child. Even the best parents, the most attentive moms and dads, know just how quickly something could go wrong, how fast the unexpected happened, especially with children. And who was to blame? The child? The parents? God? Zane had no idea, but right now he was an emotional mess. Without thinking about it, he stroked a hand through his beard. His nerves were raw at the moment. *I just have to be smart, and teach him to do the same.*

He dragged on his cigarette, letting the warm smoke billow into his lungs and holding it there for a few seconds, until he could actually feel the nicotine swimming within him. He wished it was something stronger, something that might help dull this rise in empathy. It certainly wasn't usual for him. He didn't think of himself as unfeeling or uncaring, but he was a bit of a tough guy, and for the most part he was very stoic. *I guess I'm just PMSing today or something,* he told himself and tried to laugh a little at his own sensitivity. He took another long pull on the cigarette. The smoke again filled his lungs, and he kept dragging on it so long that the filter became hot in his lips. Then, finally, he let the smoke trickle out, and leaned his head against the wall.

Car doors slammed shut near him, and from up the sidewalk he could see his next appointment approaching. Zane glanced at his phone. They were early. That was fine. He didn't have much of an appetite anyway. At least this one would be easy: a colorful floral shoulder cap consisting of roses, daisies, and peonies, something that should not disturb his currently uneasy mind. Before his clients reached him, Zane opened his phone's photo gallery and gazed at the picture of the tattoo he had just done. It was a fine piece; a piece he would have been proud to wear. The new ink was bold and bright on her skin. Zane nodded and clicked to share the photo on his social media platforms. "Beautiful portrait I had the pleasure of doing today," he posted, then clicked off his phone and greeted the couple now standing before him.

~*~

Clara lay in bed alone, utterly alone. She passed one hand over the spot next to her, the spot once occupied by her husband. After the accident, after Ben died, her husband left her, and the last bit of love and happiness she had in the world left as well. She shifted onto her side, so that one naked thigh lay on top of the blankets. She looked down from her pillow at her new tattoo, black and gray but slightly pink from inflammation. It was a beautiful portrait of her beautiful boy. But it hurt, just like the memories she was left with. Staring down at his face, caught forever at the age of five, with soft, wispy hair and big round eyes, more tears formed. They were happy and sad, and a little angry too. The tattoo burned, like a fresh, raw sunburn that had been scraped with a pumice stone. Small bubbles of ink and blood still leaked out, and they would continue to do so until her body started to mend the fresh wound. She had many wounds to heal now.

Her mind felt a little fuzzy. It was the Ambien kicking in. That and the two glasses of wine she had taken the powerful drug with. Would sleep be kind to her tonight? She thought not, but had no control as her conscious mind drifted away. She dreamt of her husband first. They were together, on the black and silver sands of Maui's Wai'anapanapa beach. After hiking through the rainforest trails and lava tubes for hours, she and her James slipped into the rich, cobalt blue water and drifted out away from the sand. It was a carefree time, a honeymoon, a time of great joy and feverish love. That very night, after the lights went out and the tourists turned down, Clara and James snuck out of their cabin in the state park and walked down to the water's edge. Clara had never had fantasies that were especially erotic, nor did she have specific 'kinks' that she knew of, but she had always wanted to make love on the beach, with the sound of the ocean in her ears, and a man that she loved atop her. That night, under a sky of a billion glittering stars, she fulfilled that fantasy.

Nine and a half months later, their son Ben was born. Her dreams shifted from long, lust-filled nights with her new husband, to a beautiful baby boy who loved to be nestled up close to her at night.

Before she knew it, Ben was walking for the first time, wobbling as if his feet were too big for his body. He rode a tricycle, bright red metal with a white seat. It even had a little bell on the handle bars he could ring. He zipped all around the driveway and on the sidewalks in front of their house. Then, his fifth birthday party, and Clara tossed in her sleep. *No, no more,* she begged, but the party continued. Then it was the next day, *the* day.

Ben ran out of the house. It was cool and he wore a dark blue cable-knit sweater. He was headed for the road. There was a great big pile of leaves there that James had raked out of the yard before the birthday party. He was smiling. He even laughed a little as he ran.

The car was already coming down the street. It was a brown Dodge Dart with rusting wheel wells and flaking paint. It approached silently and Clara could even see the driver. He was a big man with dark hair and chubby cheeks. His dark eyes stared ahead, ignorant or apathetic to Clara's terror, to Ben in the road, thrashing in the great pile of leaves. Clara ran for Ben. She would grab him, she would save him this time, but for every step she took, the shitty brown car with its dark passenger sped up. She was almost there, she could almost reach him, she just needed a second, a second out of her life to save someone else's.

With a subconscious jolt that literally lifted her from the bed, Clara woke. She was drenched with sweat. Her chest was heaving. It was still dark in her room; the clock on her bedside table read 3:05am. *Christ*. Clara brushed matted hair away from her face and tried to slow her breathing. She squeezed her eyes shut and opened them again. They were burning, not just with seasonal allergies, but with salty tears, harsh and acidic little things that burned lines down her face. Sometimes she thought she could see the tears even when they weren't there.

After a few more deep breaths, Clara lay back down against her pillow. *Ugh, gross*, it was cold and soggy with sweat. She didn't want to lay against that, even if it was her own filth. She reached next to her and tried to pull one of her extra pillows over toward her. She was met with resistance and a strange whine. Clara froze and stared down at the pillow she was holding. The bedroom was dark, but not black; she could see shades of gray. As her eyes tried to figure out what she was seeing, Clara couldn't breathe. There was something in the bed with her, something small and dark. It was moving around.

"What in the hell—" Breathless, she watched the small form sit up, and a human silhouette took shape in front of her. *Oh my god, oh my god oh my god...*

"Momma? What are you doing?" The voice was small and light, high pitched and groggy with sleep, but it was a voice she would recognize anywhere. It was her son; it was Ben.

~*~

Zane tried to get a good night's sleep, but it just wasn't in the cards for him. He had worked until 6 pm in the tattoo shop. After Clara's portrait, he tattooed a floral piece on a woman's shoulder. It was beautiful, with bright yellows and pinks and greens, with dark black filigree snaking behind the scene to add contrast. He was happy with the work, the client was happy, and that was what being an artist was all about. His third and last tattoo of the day was a traditional portrait of a European gypsy woman, with dark eyes, a bandana about her head, and full breasts that perked up high, teasing the eyes before ending in a banner that read *Forever Young*. He didn't do a lot of traditional work—he didn't like being limited by color choice—so this tattoo was more neo-traditional, a blend of the old Sailor Jerry style tattoo and a more modern portrait style. It was sleek and sexy and had just enough traditionalism to feel nostalgic.

Since it was Wednesday night, he drove to his ex-wife's house to pick up their son. Graham was a rambunctious five-year-old boy with short blonde hair and bright blue eyes. They were his mother's eyes, but the rest of him was one hundred percent Zane, from his almost perfectly round head, to the mischievous smile always on his face. He bounced to the door of his mother's mobile home to meet his father. Jaelyn was just behind Graham, holding the boy's TMNT backpack in one hand and her phone in the other. She hardly looked up at Zane when she handed him the bag.

"Not a lot of sweets tonight, Z; he's had really bad diarrhea since lunch."

Zane frowned. "Did you talk to his doctor?"

Jaelyn sighed and slipped her phone into the back pocket of her pink jeans. "It's just a stomach bug Zane, don't lose your shirt over it."

It was funny, he thought, looking at her now, with a face that was half *fuck me* hot and half bitchy, that her *feistiness*, as he used to think of it, was one of the things that had initially attracted him. Now it just pissed him off, her willful indifference, her snide texts when Zane posted on Facebook about his life's troubles. Honestly, he couldn't stand the woman. Graham jumped up and down until Zane picked him up. He squeezed the boy tightly against his large chest. Jaelyn leaned over and kissed the boy's head.

"See you tomorrow, Graham Cracker," she said.

"God Jay, you've got to stop calling him that," Zane said, shaking his head.

"Shut up, Zane," Jaelyn said and turned back away.

Graham smacked him on the chest playfully. "Yeah, shut up daddy!"

Zane heard Jaelyn giggle as she closed the door on them.

Bitch, he thought.

"You don't say that Graham. Shut up is a naughty word," he told his son as they walked out to the Jeep.

"But Mommy says it to you."

"I know, sometimes grown-ups make mistakes too."

"So who is Mommy's boss then?" Graham asked.

"I have no idea, buddy," Zane replied, then opened the back door for Graham. After he got the little one settled into his booster, Zane focused and reset himself, willing the venom out of his veins. "So, ice cream?" he asked with a twinkle of mischief in his eyes.

"Yes!" Graham screamed.

Zane nodded and climbed in, leaving his ex-wife's trailer for the last time. Bedtime was later when Graham stayed with Dad, but by nine o'clock, Graham was in misery. The diarrhea that had started early that afternoon got worse, a lot worse. Graham had shit through his clothes and then the extra set of clothes that Jaelyn had packed for him. Zane's girlfriend, Angela, was supposed to come over and spend the night, but Zane warned her off. He had enough on his plate with Graham being sick, and if it was something contagious he didn't want to spread it to Angela as well.

It was fine, she said, and she promised to come by in the morning to check on them. Graham really liked Angela. Everyone did. Well, everyone except Jaelyn. They would do breakfast in the morning, Angela had said. Zane told her that would be good. He was sure that Graham would be feeling better by then.

He wasn't getting better though, every five minutes the boy was running to the bathroom. He called the emergency nurse at his physician's office and she told him to give Graham Gatorade and take him to the ER.

Zane pulled at his beard until it hurt, trying to center his thoughts as they wove through the city to the hospital. The med-center on his side of town closed at ten. *Idiotic,* he thought, so they had to go through downtown to the south side of the city. Graham was barely awake in the back seat, sipping on a Cool Blast Gatorade from the Shell gas station. The emergency room wasn't very busy, thank God. The smell of Pine Sol and antiseptic was thick in the fluorescent lit building, and Graham's shoes squeaked against the tile floors. Zane didn't like hospitals much, not out of any particular fear, maybe it was just because he only went to them if something bad was happening.

The doctor was a middle-aged Asian man with an accent that made it difficult to understand him. The doctor seemed aware of this, though, and he spoke slowly. Graham had contracted a bacterial infection in his intestines. It was strange, the doctor said, that the symptoms just began today, because the infection was severe. Bacteria were essentially eating his guts. Graham was given antibiotics and fluids intravenously and blood was taken, vials and vials of it. Zane was a tattoo artist, he wasn't afraid of needles, but by the third time his son was being poked, he started to get angry. Angry and frustrated and hurt. *Why hadn't Jaelyn brought him to the doctor earlier? Was she lying to him about the symptoms only starting today?* Why did they have to poke so many damn holes in his son's arm? He tried to question Graham about how he had been feeling over the last few days, but the boy was barely coherent. He was delirious from exhaustion and dehydration. Graham's hospital bed was piled high with warming blankets to try to combat the chill from the intravenous fluids.

At midnight, the second time Zane had the pleasure of calling Graham's mother, the doctor decided to admit the boy. That meant it was serious, and despite the vague, quasi-reassuring responses from their attending physician, Zane was starting to freak out. The hospital staff set Graham up in a nice private room with a large bed, a reclining sofa, and a television. Graham lapsed into sleep almost instantaneously. Zane stood over his son and stroked the boy's face. His skin was pale and a little sticky to the touch. Zane tried to breathe through the emotion, but he couldn't stop the tears that welled up and over his eyelids. This was not, could not, be his sweet boy. His skin felt like a package of chicken breasts inside plastic wrap, cool and damp, and drained of life. He continued to touch Graham's face, then pet his head, stroking his hands over the short blonde hair. He watched the machine next to Graham's bed, reading his vitals. They hadn't changed at all, as far as he could tell, and the bags of fluids that hung above him on the bed still had plenty left, so Zane sat down on the recliner and put his feet up.

Though his mind was filled with a growing din of worry, sleep crept up on him. It was a sleep haunted by worry and filled with fear. He was tattooing in his sleep, as he always seemed to be, one of the downsides of the job he supposed, always thinking about work even when he was not awake. He dreamed about his last client, a tall, thin ginger with curling blondish-red hair and pale white skin that took ink extremely well. Zane was tattooing the sexy gypsy woman on his bicep. Only they weren't alone. There was someone else in his small, white booth. Zane stopped tattooing and looked over his shoulder. There was a large man… just there. He had a shiny face and pitch black hair slicked back over his scalp. His dark eyes observed Zane carefully, the irises almost indiscernible from the pupils.

"What are you doing in my booth?" Zane asked.

"I'm watching you, of course."

Zane turned back to his client, who was resting his head back and not paying attention to them at all.

"Who are you?"

The man rested a fat palm on Zane's shoulder. His skin was heavily tanned and he had an Italian look about him, like one of those old mafia bosses. Perhaps it was the chunky gold rings on the man's fingers that made Zane think so.

"You know who I am," the man answered him, and Zane looked deep into his eyes.

They were so dark, and Zane could feel himself getting lost in them. He didn't like having the man there, didn't like him staring at him that way. Zane shifted, hoping the man would remove his hand from his shoulder; instead, he leaned in closer.

"Sorry, but you have to leave. No one else is allowed in the booth while I'm working with a client."

"Oh Zane, don't be such a worrier," the man said. "I just want to see how you like my new ink."

Zane glanced down at his machine, which was loaded with the new Puritan Black. He was using the black ink on the banner beneath the beautiful gypsy, the banner that read *Forever Young*.

"*Your* new ink?"

Zane was confused. "This came from Immortal Ink," he argued, gesturing with his machine. He was getting tired of this game, whatever it was. He would never get through this tattoo if this weirdo didn't leave, and he had to finish up so that he could leave early to meet his son.

"Too right, my son," the big man said and laughed, slapping Zane's back. "I work for Immortal Ink, of course. I'm the new Ink Chef, and this new black is my recipe, my baby, I suppose you could say. Made it from my own blood, sweat, and tears." The man's eyes shimmered a little as he spoke.

"Oh… I really do have to get this finished."

"Of course you do, you have to pick up your son tonight, don't you?"

"I-yes, how did you know that?"

"Because I know you Zane, of course. You brought me here, don't you remember?"

Zane didn't remember, but the man started to back out of his booth.

"I'll let you finish your tattoo, Zane. it's looking good. Remember that great art can really come to life."

Zane nodded at the man.

"I'll see you soon Zane."

A loud buzzing woke Zane, ripping him from sleep like a Band-Aid tearing off a fresh wound. It was the machine next to Graham's hospital bed.

~*~

Aiden left the tattoo shop after his appointment feeling a little high on pain. That was just adrenaline, he knew, pumping into his system from his adrenal glands, helping his body cope with the pain of the tattoo. It was a beautiful tattoo of a sexy gypsy woman with dark, Eastern European features and huge boobs that filled up her chest. She had chocolate-colored eyes and light brown lips tinged with red. *So sexy*, he thought. It was a shame to put a shirt over her, but he was going out tonight, and he didn't want any sweaty bodies rubbing up against the fresh wound when he went to the club.

Aiden sent a few texts to his friends and told them to meet him out at the Q nightclub, which was only a few miles away. He drove fast through the city, taking every turn hard in his Subaru Impresa. Wednesday night was ladies' night at the Q, and he was in the mood to meet some honeys. There was a line outside the club, of course–there was always a line–but it wasn't as bad then as it would be at ten or eleven that night. As it was, he was getting to the club early–it was only seven o'clock–but that gave him more time to hunt for women. He waited fifteen minutes to get into the club. On a busier night, they may not have even let him in. Aiden wasn't a baller by any means, and they could tell from his attire. His clothes weren't bad, but they were from Kohl's, not an expensive boutique shop.

Bass pumping through the club bumped inside Aiden's chest, filling him up. It made his chest tight but his steps lighter, as if he were bouncing on the moon instead of walking into a sweaty nightclub. He glanced down at his smart watch. There was a group text from his friends. They weren't going to make it tonight; he was on his own. Aiden shrugged off the disappointment. He slid up to the end of the bar where the servers came in and out, and hollered over to one of the bartenders. Ordering a whiskey sour, he carried the drink with him, sipping at the tart beige liquid.

Aiden edged around tables and made his way over to where the beautiful people danced. He wasn't one of those. He was an average guy with an average job and some average clothes. But even so, he could still get lucky now and again. When the women started drinking and dancing and having fun, everything looked different to them, and average Aiden, with his freckled face and quick sense of humor, could usually score a cute girl by the end of the night.

Aiden smiled as he watched and absently brushed at his arm, then grimaced. The freshly tattooed skin throbbed as if someone had scrubbed the skin with a wire brush. He rolled his head around and took a long swig from his drink. It didn't take long for the hard liquor to kick in, and soon his vision was swimming a little and he felt lighter than ever, swaying gently to the music and watching all the legs and breasts and swirling hair on the dance floor.

Then *she* emerged. She walked out from the dancing people like a lone rider emerging from a bank of fog, and she was coming right toward him. Aiden didn't know what song was playing, but it was fast and heavy with bass. A female rapper blew furious verses too fast for his slowing mind to decipher, and he didn't try... because she was still walking toward him. She was nearly as tall as Aiden, probably five foot eight, with skinny jeans that hugged her legs all the way down to a pair of patent leather boots. The jeans rose up over her hips and hung there, just below her bellybutton, which Aiden could see because her top was cropped high, a white linen that stretched over her large breasts. Aiden couldn't take his eyes off her. Her tall body was getting closer, and he followed the swell of her breasts up to a thin, angular face. She wore a gold chain around her neck that caught the lights of the club and glittered. Her hair was black, impossibly black, cut just above her shoulders, and she wore large golden hoops in her earlobes.

The woman reached the edge of the dance floor, steps away from Aiden. She took another two steps and Aiden could see her eyes, smoky with a metallic gray eyeshadow, the corners pulled out and away with perfect stripes of eyeliner. Her skin was a thick olive which he could see even through the fog of his intoxicated mind and the flashing of lights around them. Dark caramel irises captured Aiden and held him there, lost in their beauty. She was close enough for Aiden to smell her; the scent was sweet with just a hint of musk. She reached out to him, touching his arm. A shiver startled him and he almost dropped his eight-dollar drink.

"I want you," she told him in an accent that was unmistakably European, but one that he could not easily identify.

Aiden stuttered for a moment, but then righted himself enough to speak. "You want to dance?" he asked, trying to smooth out the nervousness in his voice. She was just too damn hot, too perfect, and Aiden found himself looking down from her face and into her shirt, at the two heaving breasts there.

"I don't want to dance, Aiden." Taking his hand, she pulled him away from the dance floor, across the club. Aiden downed the last of his drink and dropped the plastic cup onto the floor. He was entranced by her as she led him. Her butt was the perfect size for squeezing while still looking firm, and Aiden's eyes never left it as he followed her. She led him to the darkest part of the club, where the VIP rooms waited.

A big man—tall with a large belly—stood in front of the hallway to the VIP section. His hair was shiny and black, combed straight back from his forehead. When Aiden approached, the man stared at him and a wide smile crept over his round face. The woman touched the man on his arm and he moved out of the way. Aiden didn't like the way the bouncer stared at him while they passed, but then the mysterious woman turned and smiled back at him, and Aiden's insides went mushy once more. Well, some parts didn't. She led him down the corridor. He had never been into the VIP wing, but she seemed to know exactly where she was going. It crossed Aiden's mind that she could be a prostitute, but he didn't give a shit. The hallway was hazy with cigarette smoke. There was no smoking allowed in the club, but that must be one of the perks of being a VIP.

Almost at the end of the hallway, the woman turned and pressed down the handle of a steel door. It opened before her and she led Aiden into a room with a long, red leather couch against the wall and two red leather loveseats on either side of it. A coffee table with an ice bucket sat in the middle of the room. There was a bottle of something in it. *Must be champagne*, he thought. *That's what they drink in these rooms, isn't it?* The woman pulled him in and closed the door. Once the latch clicked, she pressed herself into his chest, and Aiden's heart thumped against her large breasts. She leaned her face in close to him, and brushed her lips across his.

Aiden let out a stuttering breath. His cheeks were hot, and probably red, his ginger skin betraying every blush. She flicked her tongue out, tasting his lips. She tasted like whiskey and cigarettes, a combination he was surprised to find incredibly sexy. She breathed out against him, then drew him over to the red couch, pressing him down. Aiden flopped onto the couch and sank into the rich leather. Her eyes were so dark, her lips so red. She swayed above him for a moment, her hips moving from side to side with the rhythm of the bass that bumped through the air all around them. Then she pulled her top over her head and tossed it to the floor. Her large breasts were finally exposed and Aiden let out a moan. She lowered herself down on top of him and pressed her mouth onto his. It was wet and he was ready.

"What's your name?" he asked between mouthfuls of her.

"You know who I am, silly man; I'm your gypsy girl." Then her hands reached down and began unbuttoning his pants. Aiden leaned his head back as she continued to undress him, her lips and teeth nipping at his neck while her hands did wonderful things down below. On his upper arm, his tattoo continued to throb along with his heartbeat, and droplets of blood and Puritan Black seeped out of the fresh artwork and dribbled down his arm.

~*~

Jasmine Ives woke up on Thursday morning feeling amazing. There was soft, white light filtering in through her blinds and the air was rich with a very pleasant aroma. She felt next to her on the bed. Matthew wasn't there. Jasmine frowned, he must be up and showering. She rose slowly from bed, stretching her arms out wide, letting her muscles open up and breathe after a long night of sleep. She rotated her torso, gently popping her back, then leaned forward and back. She felt good, great actually.

Jasmine slipped out of bed and padded to the bathroom wearing nothing but the white panties that shone brightly against her light brown skin. Matthew wasn't in the bathroom, but when she flipped on the light a smile rose on her face. On the bathroom counter was a vase filled with a large bouquet of flowers. It was their sweetness which she had smelled all the way from her bed. They were beautiful, with bright greens and pinks and yellows. There were spindly black curly sticks placed in between the flowers. She smiled even larger and thought she might cry at the sight.

What a wonderful gift, she thought. Jasmine turned to the side a little and looked at herself in the mirror. Her new tattoo was vibrant in the morning light, daisies and roses and peonies. Even the black filigree was sharp and bold, just like the sticks and flowers in the vase. Matthew had really outdone himself, first buying her the tattoo, and then getting her a bouquet that matched it perfectly. *Sneaky little bugger, how did he do that?* She was still smiling as she sat down on the toilet. Matthew would be getting something extra special tonight, she decided.

Jasmine left the bathroom and pulled on a long sleeve T-shirt, then went out into the living room, looking for Matthew. What she saw stopped her in her tracks. The living room and dining room were covered with flowers. It was like a rainforest in her home, bright and warm and inviting. And the smell. It was sweet and full, as if she had her face right next to the flowers.

"Oh my god," she said. "Matthew! Matthew, how did you do all of this?"

The clock on the stove said it was only nine in the morning, how on earth did he get all of these flowers in here? And why? The flowers in the bathroom were sweet, but what was she going to do with all of these? The bouquets were set on every possible surface: the TV stand, the coffee table, the end tables, the small inset shelves behind the couch. The dining room table was dwarfed by one enormous bouquet, with flowers so large they couldn't possibly be real. But as she approached the table and took one daisy petal gently in her hand, she felt that it was genuine. *But how?* Wandering into the kitchen, there were more flowers everywhere, consuming her counter space. *What on earth?* There was a note hanging on the fridge for her. She recognized Matthew's pharmacist scrawl immediately.

Hey baby, I had to leave early for work, but I love you. See you tonight, Matthew. Also, what's up with all the flowers in here?

What's up with all the flowers? What did he mean? she thought, reading the note again. *Did he not bring the flowers? If he didn't bring the flowers, who did?*

~*~

Zane was in full panic mode. Three nurses were running down the hospital ward, pushing Graham on his bed as they went. Double doors ahead of them opened, and then they turned and more doors appeared for them to go through. Zane ran alongside them, his ragged breaths stuttering in and out of him. He felt lightheaded, and the strong smell of ammonia filled his nostrils so that every breath felt like it was burning down his airways. The last set of doors opened slowly, a surgical suite. The medical team pushed Graham through. Zane tried to follow but one of the nurses stopped him with a firm hand against his chest.

Something clicked off in his brain and Zane unleashed on the young man, screaming and shoving the nurse. Zane was a big guy, and he thought he would topple through the thin nurse, but the man stood firm. Zane smelled soap as he was smashed up against the man, who was calling for help with a small black communication device hanging around his neck. Then more arms were on him, dragging Zane away from the surgical suite and from his son. Zane fought against them all, swinging his arms wildly.

"You have to let me in there, you have to let me see my son! You can't do this!"

The nurses were talking to Zane, trying to calm him, but it was all a mushy blur. Then a woman started screaming. He recognized the voice, it was his ex, running up the hallway toward them.

"What's happening, what did you do Zane? Where is my son?" Jaelyn's high-pitched voice had reached hysterical levels.

Jaelyn crashed into the pile of men and women in front of the surgical suite and added her body weight to the fight. It was a mess of sweat and swearing and crying.

Then a booming male voice yelled, "Stand back! Code 43!"

At once the hands grappling with Zane released, and he turned toward the new voice, confused. Jaelyn did as well. A dark-clad security officer stood a few yards from them down the hall. Zane opened his mouth to speak, but as he did so, a yellow spark shot out from whatever the officer was carrying and Zane felt an explosion of pain in his chest. A fire lit up in his skin and raged through his entire body. He shook, and writhed, and then, finally, he fell to the floor. It was silent for a moment, on the floor, but he woke into another nightmare.

Zane was back in the tattoo booth. He was gloved, holding a machine. There was someone in his chair; a large man with a big belly and black, greasy hair. He smelled like Vaseline, sweet and disgusting at the same time. The man smiled at him. His teeth were straight and white, while his eyes were the opposite, small black holes in his head.

"Welcome back, my man!" the large man said to him.

Zane stared at him without talking or moving. He didn't know what he was supposed to be doing here, didn't know why this man was back.

"I have to go; my son is in the hospital."

The man laughed.

"No, he's not, Zane," he said, and a wide grin took up his face, making him look more reptilian than human. "He's here with me now."

Graham appeared beside the man, pale and sickly—just as he had been when Zane brought him to the hospital.

"Graham, how did you get here?"

Graham tried to speak but the large man put a hand on his shoulder and shook his head. "He's no longer your concern, Zane."

With that, the man stood, and in his dark eyes Zane could see a fire burning, hot and rich, a deep red blaze within the man. He stepped close to Zane and pointed one finger out at him, in front of his chest. As Zane watched, the finger glowed, first a peachy yellow, then bright orange. It was hot, red hot, like a poker left in a fire. Then the dark man shoved it into Zane's chest, jabbing hard into his muscle.

It burned. Oh God, it burned. Zane cried out and tried to back away, but he was trapped there with his back against the wall, and the big man laughed. Zane could hear his own flesh sizzling beneath the man's finger and a smell like burnt meat filled his nose. He gagged on the smell and tried to beat away the man's hand, but now the whole thing was glowing, brighter and brighter as if the he was Johnny Fucking Storm. Pain rose and overflowed within Zane and tears burst out of his eyes. He screamed and screamed, flailing against the wall of his own tattoo booth. In the distance, in a place far away from him, he could hear the man's laughter.

Then silence, blackness, and Zane woke. He stared up at a white ceiling and tried to raise his body only to find that he was restrained. He jerked his arms but they didn't move. He looked around. He was on a hospital bed with his arms bound by his side. The room was bright, with curtains pulled closed all around him, separating him from the rest of…wherever he was.

"Zane," a familiar female voice said.

"Yes," he answered, and his voice caught a little in his throat. It was hoarse and hurt to speak. "Oh god, what happened? Why do I hurt so bad?"

Jaelyn rose from the short plastic chair she had been sitting in. Her eyes were dark and adorned with deep red bags. She looked very ill, and very tired.

"Security hit you with a Taser, Zane, and your heart stopped."

"My heart, what?" he croaked.

"You were unresponsive. They resuscitated you, but had to shove a tube down your throat to get you breathing again." Her voice was flat and dead, no trace of her usual snottiness.

"Christ," he muttered. Well, that was why his throat hurt so bad. "Where is Graham, is he okay?"

Jaelyn stared him down, her eyes revealing no emotion. "Graham died during surgery, Zane. That's the only reason I stayed, to tell you that."

Her words seemed to bounce right off of him, they didn't stick, they didn't sink in. "Wait, where is he?" Zane asked.

"He's dead, Zane. They said there was an infection in his gut and his intestines got twisted up, gastroenteritis.

His intestines burst and sent the infection everywhere. His body couldn't fight it."

The way she spoke was so mechanical, so cold, that Zane hardly recognized it.

"That's all I have to say," Jaelyn said, and turned away from his bed. She parted the curtain and left Zane alone to grapple with what he had just heard.

It wasn't possible, was it? Graham was a healthy boy. He had just had a well-child visit with his pediatrician and he came out perfectly healthy, "a normal, rambunctious boy," the physician had said. Jaelyn had not been gone for five minutes before a man in blue scrubs entered Zane's little room.

"Is it true?" Zane asked the man.

The man regarded him carefully. Zane had already shown his propensity for violent outbursts. He glanced behind him as if to see if he had any backup, then cleared his throat.

"Graham passed away about an hour ago. He suffered a major rupture in his intestine, which flooded his body with toxic, necrotic tissue. I'm sorry, sir."

Zane nodded his head as a numbness spread through him. This couldn't be real, it had to be some kind of fucked up nightmare. He would wake up at any time.

"Because of the intense emotional strain you were under, the hospital has decided not to press charges for assault." The doctor paused and cleared his throat again. "However, we must insist that if you are in need of medical care, you seek attention elsewhere. Do you understand?"

Zane understood, and he also didn't. How could his son be dead? How could this have happened? Zane's stomach churned and a sick heat built up inside him.

"Am I free to go then?" he asked. His scratchy voice sounded hollow even in his own head.

"Yes, I just need you to sign a few forms," the man said. "Someone will be contacting you regarding his final arrangements."

~*~

Two hours later, Zane unlocked his Jeep and forced himself into the driver's seat. He looked over his shoulder. Graham's empty booster seat was back there. Zane didn't know what to do or where to go, so he smoked cigarettes and drove aimlessly through the city. The seatbelt pressed against his bruised chest, so he flung it off, not caring what happened to him if he was in a collision. Several times, he stopped at intersections and just sat there, waiting for some kind of direction, but getting none. His stomach gurgled. He was nauseated, but his stomach was empty. He hadn't eaten since last night, and it was now after noon. It seemed like an insane thing to think about right now. How could he think about feeding himself when he had just learned his son was dead? *Dead.* Again, Zane paused in an intersection, tears pouring down his face. What a strange sight he must be; a thirty-five-year-old man, tattooed all the way up to his lower jaw, with large eyelets in his ears, bawling his eyes out whilst sitting at a stop sign. What a cruel bitch this life was.

To his left, a man began to cross the street. He was a large man, with a big belly and black hair that was slicked back in oily lines against his scalp. He strode into the street with long, slow strides, almost as if he were savoring the steps, really enjoying the journey. The man turned his head toward Zane, and Zane saw a familiar wide, white-toothed smile. The man's eyes were dark, his skin crinkled up while he looked at Zane.

As Zane watched with his mouth open and eyes wide, the man lifted one hand and gave him a thumbs up. Zane's dumbfoundedness lasted another moment before rage took over. It was his fault. Somehow this man had something to do with Graham's death. He started to lift his foot off the brake, ready to jam it onto the accelerator and crush the fat man, but then a loud *honk* broke his concentration.

Zane looked in the rearview mirror to see a small Ford Focus right up his ass. The driver laid on the horn again, and Zane could see him waving his hands madly in frustration. He didn't give a shit. He turned his attention back to the crosswalk, to the man who wasn't there. Zane craned his neck looking up and down the street, but there was no sign of his dark-haired antagonist. Zane turned in the direction he saw the man go.

After two blocks, he saw the large man again. There was no way he could have walked so far so fast, but Zane continued his pursuit. As soon as he neared his quarry, the man left the sidewalk and walked up a concrete path to a small yellow house nestled in between a brown brick home and a slightly decrepit-looking blue one. The man walked up onto a covered porch and then opened the door to the house. Before he entered, the man looked over his shoulder at Zane, who was just pulling up outside the house. He winked at Zane and then entered the house, leaving the door open behind him.

Zane jammed the Jeep in between two cars on the opposite side of the street and ran across. His heart was beating hard and his breaths were short, but still he sprinted up the walking path to the porch. Zane didn't hesitate even for a moment; he ran right in through the open doorway. A thick, flowery smell struck Zane when he entered the house, the kind of smell one might experience if they walked into a greenhouse full of spring flowers. Then he gave pause. There was no sign of the dark-haired man, but he heard someone in the house. He inched further in, and the smell of flowers grew stronger. He walked into the main living space and was assaulted by bouquets of flowers all around, bright and fragrant. They looked... familiar.

A woman walked into the room. She saw Zane and screamed, then backed away quickly, smacking into a wall and sliding down a little. He recognized her, then she recognized him. It was a client he had tattooed the day before.

"Zane? What the hell are you doing here?" she asked, in a voice that was partly a gasp and partly a cry.

"I—I," Zane stumbled on his words. What the hell was he doing here? In someone else's house? "I was following someone and he came in here. The door was open." His words came out flat, his tongue feeling like a piece of cardboard.

Jasmine straightened herself back up from the wall. She was wearing a t-shirt and panties but nothing else. Zane felt very uncomfortable standing there. "There's nobody here but me, and you can't just walk into my house!"

"No, I—I saw him, it was a big man with dark hair. He walked right in here."

The woman's eyes narrowed. "There is no one else here, and you shouldn't be here either."

Zane nodded, feeling more dumbfounded than ever. Could he be hallucinating? Was he having some kind of psychotic break? "Sorry," he mumbled, and turned away to leave.

"Wait, Zane."

He turned back to her and now she eyed him with curiosity.

"Did you send me all these flowers?" Jasmine asked. "I thought my husband did, but he has no idea where they came from. You're the only other person who knows about my new tattoo."

"What? Why would I send you flowers? What do they have to do with your tattoo?"

"Because they match," she said, turning to the side so he could see the fresh ink.

Zane stared at the tattoo, and slowly it dawned on him that she was right. He looked from the tattoo to the flowers that had erupted all over the house. They were a perfect match. He shook his head a little, thinking he could clear it from his brain, but the flowers were still there, roses and daisies and peonies, yellows and pinks and greens. *What the hell is going on here?*

"I didn't send you anything," Zane said.

"You're sure?"

"Absolutely," he said, and turned away from her. He left the house feeling like he was in a dream. As he closed the door behind him, Zane gazed out over the lawn and down the street. He squinted under the glare of the sun. *I'm losing my mind, that's what's happening.* Tattoos weren't magic and they didn't make things appear. Zane walked back down toward the street, the smell of freshly cut grass in the air accompanied him. He thought about his dream, or vision, or whatever it was, where the large man was in his booth with him. What had the man said?

"Great art comes to life…" he murmured, then crossed the street to his Jeep. There was something gnawing at his mind, something he couldn't quite nail down yet. *The flowers, the flowers, the flowers…*

Once he was back in the Jeep and driving away, he smoked a cigarette, hitting it long and hard every time. His stomach growled at him again, reminding Zane that he needed to eat. Subs 'N Meats was on the way home. He activated his talk to text and spoke to his phone.

"I'm on my way home now. Can you come over?" The text was to his girlfriend, Angela. Seconds later she replied.

"Of course, I'll leave now."

"Thanks."

Zane pulled into Subs 'N Meats. He took a moment to compose himself, rubbing his cheeks to brush away the salty streaks his tears had left behind. Zane walked into the old brick building and was at once hit with the smells of toasted bread, sweet marinara, and a mix of peppers and onions. He inhaled deeply. The smell was rich and familiar, and for a moment, the sickly smell of the hospital was washed from his lungs. Zane ordered himself a sandwich and then a salad for Angela. He leaned on the counter, waiting, until the door chimed and a boisterous voice called out to him.

"Zane! Tattoo Zane, I've got to talk to you."

Zane turned and saw another of his tattoo clients from yesterday walking in. It was the tall, ginger kid he did the neo-trad gypsy on at the end of the day. Zane sighed, he just didn't have anything left today. He didn't want to have to pretend to care about what this kid had to say. The young man slapped Zane on the shoulder as he approached.

"Whoa man, you look down in the dumps today."

Zane's throat immediately tightened. He blinked at the boy several times, willing himself not to cry. He felt the skin of his face tremble. The kid continued to watch him, waiting for an answer, but all Zane could manage was a dry, "yeah."

"You're not going to believe what happened last night, freaking best night of my life!"

Zane was starting to feel ill. It had been the best night of his life, and the worst of Zane's. His eyes began to fill, he couldn't stop them.

"Well, you remember this," he said, pulling up his shirt cuff and revealing the fresh gypsy girl tattoo on his bicep. "Now check this shit out!"

Aiden pulled his phone out and swiped across the screen, then thrust it in front of Zane's face. "I met her up at the Q last night. Just look at her man. She's the fucking girl!"

Zane's vision, blurry from a fresh onslaught of tears, suddenly came into sharp focus as Aiden showed him the picture. It was Aiden, taking a selfie with a tall brunette. But not just any tall brunette. Aiden swiped through more photos, and Zane took in the woman's facial features, features Zane knew well since he had just tattooed them on the boy's arm not twelve hours ago. Aiden swiped to the next picture; it showed the dark-haired woman again. This time, she was taking the selfie from on top of Aiden's lap. Her shirt was off, exposing her large breasts.

The next photo was more graphic still, but Zane didn't even register it. His head was spinning, and he was having trouble seeing what was right in front of his face. He had tattooed those flowers and then they appeared in the woman's house. He had tattooed the sexy gypsy and then gingerbread here had mysteriously run into her last night at the club. His brain was filled with these thoughts, and then a disturbing and childish realization floated into his head. *I tattooed them and they really happened. I tattooed the flowers and they appeared, same with the girl. So, that must mean… the boy, the little boy. Could I have brought the kid back to life, too? What in the fuck am I thinking? I don't have magical powers, do I? Am I cursed? Is this real?*

Then the man–the large, dark man–floated into his head. Zane could smell the thick Vaseline smell of him. The man had told Zane that it was *his* special recipe of tattoo ink, Puritan Black, the very ink he had used for the first time yesterday. "Lot 187," Zane mumbled.

"What? Hey, what Zane? What did you say?" The kid with the gypsy tattoo was shaking him and Zane snapped back to reality, suddenly realizing he had completely zoned out in the middle of the restaurant. He looked up at Aiden, who was staring down at him quizzically. The boy's eyebrows pinched together.

"Are you okay man?"

Zane didn't answer. He pushed the boy to the side, hard enough to send him toppling into the pop machine. Then Zane bolted for the door. He heard someone yelling after him, but he was already through the door and barreling into the street. He nearly dove into the Jeep and sped away from Subs 'N Meats, heading toward home, fast. He was overcome with urgency, and he didn't know exactly why. He just knew he had to get there, before… before what? *Something*, and there wasn't much time.

Three more blocks, three more until I'm home. Zane took the next turn hard and kept on the accelerator. His phone buzzed in his pocket. He fished it out with one hand and flipped it over, glancing down from the road as he did so. There was a new message request from, 'Your Pal,' on the screen. The accompanying thumbnail for the number was the same thick, greasy face that had been haunting his dreams. The deep black eyes and slicked back hair filled out the rest of the dark man's features. Zane clicked on the message and it opened to show a picture. It was the large man, standing hip-to-hip with Clara, Zane's first client yesterday morning, the first one he used the new ink on. The man had an arm around her waist.

Standing between the two was Clara's son, five-year-old Ben; five-year-old Ben that Zane knew to be dead. Yet here he was, smiling, happy, and very much alive. Zane's heart was palpitating rapidly as he stared down at the image. The dark man looked so happy, with his bright white teeth and large belly stretching out his shirt. Then a loud scream broke Zane's concentration.

Zane startled and looked back up at the road just in time to see a red jacket and long, brown hair strike the front of his Jeep. There was a loud *crunch* and Zane slammed on the brakes. The Jeep fishtailed hard, sweeping back and forth before finally rocking to a halt. *Jesus Christ, what the hell did I do?* Zane climbed out of the Jeep and saw that he was right in front of his house. He had been so distracted that he'd nearly driven right by it. Something looked wrong with the house, though, and as he jogged behind the Jeep to find what he'd hit, Zane realized what it was.

When his mother passed away eight years ago, Zane had planted a willow tree in his front yard in remembrance of her. Willows had always been her favorite, and every day when Zane left the house and saw the tree growing, blooming, thriving, he was reminded of his mother. In a way, it helped him feel like she was still out there, still alive in some other plane of existence. *Not anymore.* The tree was a husk of what it had been yesterday, a gnarled, brown mess of limbs and trunk.

All dead, all gone. Understanding came then, the cold bitch that it was. Zane approached the place where the wide smear of blood ended, and saw the lump of hair and blood and clothes on the ground. *I tattooed the flowers and my mother's tree died, I tattooed the child and my own son died, which means… the girl.*

Zane fell to his knees by the wreckage of the body he had hit. He grabbed a handful of long, brown hair, hair that he himself had snuggled his face into on so many nights. Zane turned the head toward him, and Angela's hazel eyes rolled up, staring past him, still and lifeless. Locked onto her face was an expression of surprise. Zane held Angela's head in his lap and sat back on his heels. He stared up at the sky, fresh tears streaming down his face.

~*~

In a cold, stone room, a large, dark man sat at a desk that was too small for his body, humming quietly to himself. He poured thick, black liquid from a graduated cylinder into three smooth-sided bottles. Then he set the glass cylinder down and picked up a needle. Delicately, he inserted the needle into the thumb of his left hand. He didn't wince as the needle passed through the layers of his skin and struck a thin capillary below. Setting the needle down, he squeezed his thumb over the three ink bottles, letting a drop of blood splash into each. Then he capped the bottles, and over each one he affixed a label with a familiar black silhouette on its face. Under the bold title of Puritan Black was another line of text that read, 'Lot No. 188.'

~*~

Devour

P.K. Tyler

~*~

Research Notes of Dr. Chaya Nasrati

Extensive research into the parasitical nature of viruses has, naturally, resulted in a dead end. Any proof of Dimmock's degeneracy hypothesis has been lost to the annals of time. Researchers insisting the existence of bacteria such as rickettsia and chlamydia prove the ability of a microorganism to evolve from parasitism have lost their focus. The question is not, Which box can we fit the virus into, *but* how do I build a new box?

The existence of the virus is, in itself, proof of the existence of God. Neither sentient nor self-sustaining, the genetic component of the viral makeup indicates, to this researcher at least, that there is something to be learned from an organism which is neither life nor inanimate. We must push ourselves to think beyond the limits of animal, mineral, and vegetable. The three-domain construct is, by its very nature, flawed.

We know there are organisms which can exist in either an independent state or in conjunction with another life form. We know that cells, diseases, and bacteria don't care which domain a host entity falls into. The scientific community's refusal to look for something older by which to classify life is simple ignorance and hubris.

The CDC's refusal to allow my plasmidial research on the basis of ethical concerns has forced my hand. And so, as true innovation must always do, I forge ahead alone.

~*~

Amina Foxx
Stage 3
CDC Alerted – Awaiting Pickup
KGR-13 ND#7431

Amina moaned as she woke. The pain in her back had receded to a dull ache, but the glaring light seared through her brain whether her eyes were open or closed.

She couldn't remember how long she'd been here; even her name eluded her. The pain, which had been her constant companion for so many weeks, blurred out all rational thought. Instead of thinking about her job and the days of work she had missed, she spent moment to moment in a quest to alleviate her agony.

White-blue light greeted her as she awoke, blinding her and making her lift an arm over her face.

The motion distracted her from the ice pick of light boring into her brain and brought her attention to the convulsion lashing through her shoulder. A scream ripped from her dry lips, an alien sound consisting of a gurgling, guttural voice Amina did not recognize as her own.

Muscles screamed as she pulled her aching body up into a sitting position, each movement ripping through her muscles and nerves. As the sheet fell away from her body, she felt as if something was peeling her skin away in slow, methodical movements. Sandpaper scraped against every surface of her skin. After an agonizing show of endurance, Amina rested back against her pillows, eyes still closed.

Falling back into what she prayed would be a more comfortable position, Amina moaned again. The desired relief did not appear. The cool air chilled her; the delicate skin on her arms prickled with goose pimples, flesh pulling against the atrophying sinew connecting it to her body.

She opened and closed her mouth, unable to form clear enough thoughts to realize she was thirsty. Dry and cracking skin broke her lips, the flesh around her mouth discolored and sore. One of the many enigmas about this disease was that the patients seemed to be dying of dehydration even as their bodies oozed fluids without restraint.

The light behind Amina's eyelids dimmed, allowing her a momentary reprieve. Sighing, she lifted a hand, cautiously this time, without knowing what she reached for. Pain and thirst twisted her mind, leaving her moaning and thrashing in pain.

"Amina?" A muted voice shot spikes into her head. Light slashed through the darkness, illuminating the figure across the room. Amina's body reacted to the light. She rolled to the side and pulled her head as far away from the invasion as possible.

"Amina?" he repeated, closing the door. Eric Foxx expected some kind of reaction from the husk named Amina. She moaned and, lolled her head toward the sound, a small movement compared to before. The brain learns quickly to minimize actions that cause pain.

The person spoke again. "Baby, are you in here?"

Amina's eyes burned, forcing her to close them. Thick mucus ran down her face, pooling in her ears where it blended with another, darker fluid that dripped from her inner ear. Tubes connected to her body, blood thinners, and saline, plus other untested drugs that may or may not slow the progression of the disease. No one knew the final outcome.

Amina had been one of the first outside the large cities to become ill. Her work had taken her to New York City just before the CDC announced a spreading contagion and warned people to wear masks and gloves whenever in large crowds. In the beginning, when she sneezed, she attributed it to the usual spring cold. She didn't connect it with her trip or the increasing number of stories on the news about the burgeoning pandemic.

Now everyone she knew, everyone she had touched or stood next to on an elevator, had been exposed. By association, everyone they knew suffered. So far, little hope of a cure remained.

Rumors spread in Flushing, Queens of a man who had made a complete recovery after receiving an antiviral medication for meningitis, but no one could verify or repeat the results. A hospital in Wichita claimed to have cured an ill child by introducing small amounts of mercury into her system. But the child soon died from the poison so many had hoped would cure her.

The light dimmed again, and Amina sighed in relief. The stinging blue glow had been her constant companion. Now, without the initial intensity, Amina could endure the pounding in her head. Thoughts tangled her mind, unable to congeal into coherent meaning beyond minimizing pain and seeking relief for the burning in her throat.

"Fadlik," Amina moaned, speaking in the mother tongue which she had not used in twenty years. "Fadlik, Ummi…"

"Amina, baby, I'm here…"

Eric Foxx rushed into the dark room containing his wife. She was one of three patients crammed into a small triage room. It should not have been used for admitted patients, but there was nowhere else for them to go. The hospital overflowed with the sick, both real and hypochondriacs who feared infection.

The number of infected had escalated, and no one could get accurate information from the CDC anymore if you reached them at all. Nine days had passed since the hospital admitted Amina and she barely received enough treatment to keep her alive. Or maybe she received all the treatment anyone could offer.

Eric had met his wife during the first Gulf War. She was too young to realize falling in love with a white American soldier would end any ties she had with her Kuwaiti family. Still, Amina had always been strong, stronger than any of the women he'd ever encountered. Strong enough to challenge his heart and mind and always win.

When they met, Eric was twenty-three and Amina seventeen—too young for marriage by American standards. With the consent of her mother, they wed in Kuwait, and she came to America as his wife. The day after they left her home, she had received a call from her older brother. Her mother had been punished for going against their father's wishes by allowing Amina to wed an *alshit'an a'bi*. She died in a small medical clinic three days later.

Amina never again spoke Arabic or mentioned her family unless an unsuspecting acquaintance asked her about them. Few people asked a second time. Eric's wife had a quick and vicious sense of humor few wanted aimed at them. It was one of the things he loved most about her—she never ceased to surprise him with the way her mind worked; she was insightful and cutting.

Eric sped across the dim room, maneuvering around the cots and IV stands. He couldn't imagine how the nurses managed to get close enough to the patients to take care of them. Between the overworked staff and overcrowded patients, conditions in the hospital plummeted. Soon, instead of being a safe haven from disease, it would become an incubator.

The room smelled of cleaning solution, sweat, and another, more primal and less recognizable scent. It singed the hairs in Eric's nose and forced him to breathe through his mouth.

At the foot of Amina's bed, Eric made out the shape of his wife and heard her soft moans. The light from the hall filtered in through Venetian blinds, providing the illusion of privacy in a public place.

"Ummi," she moaned, startling Eric.

"Mina, baby…I'm right here…" he took a step around the edge of her bed and flicked on the small fluorescent light above her.

Her screams began just a second before his. Agony echoed in her brain as the light pierced her eyelids, scorching her retinas and dissolving the thin membrane holding her eyes together. The viscous fluid that once filled her optic organs washed down her face, leaving behind only the hollowed-out sockets.

The shocking torment reverberating within her skull dulled, and the blue light disappeared. Amina opened her lids, unaware she would not be able to see. She sat up, her body still resisting movement, but now something more important than pain held her attention.

Breathing in, she tasted something familiar in the air, something enticing that awoke an unexpected hunger.

Her guts roiled and gurgled within, begging to be filled.

Eric's screams continued as he stared, mouth agape at the form that not a day ago had been his entire world. His beautiful, exotic wife. Before him sat something barely recognizable as human. Bits of her outer layers of skin peeled off, leaving her covered in raw red and fatty yellow chunks of flesh.

A transparent membrane had formed beneath her skin, holding her organs and muscles in place. Her flesh was sloughing away and being replaced with a substance more similar to the vitelline membrane that protects the yoke inside an egg.

Moisture was the single thing that would alleviate the intense pain of patients who progressed to this stage; morphine proved ineffective even in euthanizing dosages. Water wasn't enough. They'd tried emerging patients in tubs only to find the membrane would dissolve, leaving the patient exposed to the air and infection until a new layer grew back. Untreated, the patients oozed enough fluid from their orifices and through their remaining flesh to coat them with a slick slime. This appeared the sole thing to offer relief.

Amina tilted her head, searching for the enticing smell. The pain in her body decreased as her focus sharpened. As she moved, leaning toward whatever called to her with the power of a siren's song, her muscles and skin no longer tormented her.

Eric backed away from the creature before him, unable to reconcile the monstrous creature with the beautiful woman he had married. The black holes replacing her eyes gaped at him, sludge sliding down her olive skin, discolored with the tinge of death.

"Amina?" Eric asked, his back against the window, Venetian blinds bending and snapping out of place as he pushed as far away from her as possible.

A low growl came from her as she opened her mouth, almost like she was smiling at him, if not for the stench of sulfur-emitting from her.

Eric inched toward the door, but each movement he made carried his scent through the air to the Amina-thing. She growled again, a low predatory sound, and moved forward on all fours. Her tongue flicked out, tasting his scent on the air.

Empty orbs followed his movements.

Naked and crouched like a wild animal, Amina allowed her instincts to guide her. She couldn't see. Instead, she perceived her surroundings in sharp, clearly contrasting tastes and sounds. Distinct smells surrounded her: two bodies registered as familiar, like brethren, and a third, enticing smell. The heat of Eric's body drew her in, and the taste of his skin in the air called her. He spoke, making a sound she couldn't decipher, but the cadence appealed to her.

She rocked forward a bit, her need growing, creating a near-painful cramping in her body. Whatever gave off this smell was something she craved, something she needed. She needed it to survive, to exist. It had something she did not, and without it, she would cease to be. Biology demanded she act, that she consume and absorb this thing before her.

She sprang from her crouch.

Eric fell beneath her, slipping away from her grasp. He screamed.

The vibrations excited her, her body quivering with the anticipation of something she could not name.

Eric shrieked as the distorted face of his wife sniffed at him. She held him down with a strength she'd never possessed and should not have after suffering a debilitating illness. When she inhaled against his chest and moaned, Eric's cries became frantic.

The hallway outside of Amina's room was empty; the shift changing, the nurses exhausted, and the hospital understaffed. Orderlies and technicians kept things running as best they could, but the small triage room down one hall of the ER had been forgotten in the chaos. No one heard Eric's wails except for the patients in adjacent rooms, too possessed with their own pain to register the sound as external.

A bloodcurdling howl ripped through the hospital as Amina consumed the source of her attraction. She crawled out of the room, still naked and on all fours. Eric's claret blood covered her, arterial spray coating her face and torso. She stalked down the hall, looking for another victim, someone other than her brethren who might have the same intoxicating smell. Addicted, her need overwhelmed any remaining self Amina might have retained.

The triage room door closed, leaving Eric's lifeless body on the floor in the dark antechamber. His blood pooled around him, sections of skull and gray matter lay like forgotten puzzle pieces.

In the middle bed, John Petersen sat up, inspired by the scent of nourishment. The pain in his body receded as his eyes throbbed. Desperation to relieve the pressure surged through his limbs. Pushing the heels of his hands against his face, he popped the ocular membranes. Soon, he crouched on all fours and began the search for something to relieve his hunger.

~*~

No One Will Believe You

Jessica West

~*~

"I told you no one would believe you."

Clay's hot breath stank of whiskey and cigar smoke.

Right about the same time the trap door dropped out from under my boots, a crow startled, cawing and flying off.

They say everything comes fairly easy for women. I had hoped this, in particular, would be quick. A snapped neck. Darkness. I should have known better. Nothing was ever that easy for me. I struggled. I kicked as I hanged, catching flashes of the first night he came into my room.

I died reliving the worst day of my life. But that wasn't even the worst part. Even after I couldn't move any more, couldn't breathe, I could still feel. I felt it the moment I lost control of my body and shit slid down my legs. I smelled it. *Then* everything went black.

But it didn't stay like that. The world came back gray. Like all the color had drained out and left nothing but a muddy canvas, vague shapes painted in shades that ranged from ashes to rain puddles.

The shapes moved. Blobs of dark against the pasty background seeped into my awareness like blood soaking through fabric. I couldn't feel or smell or hear anything. There was no sense of presence, no context of being. I simply *was*. I could see, after a fashion, so I focused on that.

And I could *remember*.

I saw his face in some abstract flash. Then he was there, his back to me, facing the fireplace. Sitting in my favorite chair. Ma's old chair. The green wingback Aunt Helen had given them on their wedding day.

He had his dick in his hand, his head laid back, and his trousers around his ankles.

Man's got a fuckin' problem is what it is. But you think anybody'd believe me? I was just a kid. *His* kid, but still—just a kid. I knew they'd not believe me. That's why I tried so hard to hide it for so long.

But after he married me off to Paul, I knew it was to come out. Sure enough, on our wedding night, the consummation led to a lack of blood on the sheets and lots of tears. What else could I do? I told him everything.

For a while, I thought it was gonna be okay. Paul didn't have much to say about it, but what was there to say? Every time he tried to touch me, though, I kept seeing Clay's face. I cried every time. I couldn't help it. I'd cried every time Clay fucked me and I cried when Paul tried to fuck me.

Eventually Paul told the preacher I was having visions. The preacher told the sheriff I was possessed. And now here we are.

Me dead and this asshole jerkin' his jimmy. I wonder how long I've been gone, if he even waited until they buried my corpse in the dirt.

It can't end like this.

This isn't the end, Charlotte.

Who's there? A man's voice, but not Clay's. *Where you at?*

Long story short, I can talk to ghosts. And I can help you.

Why would you help me? What's in it for you?

A soul.

Mine?

His. Yours is already condemned, but, I believe, wrongly so.

I'm confused.

That won't clear up any time soon. Maybe not ever. Do you want him to suffer?

Hold up. How's about answering some questions?

No. I make you an offer. You accept or refuse. There's nothing else to talk about.

What offer? You haven't said anything!

Do you want him to suffer?

I won't answer that. I won't say yes when I don't know what I'm agreeing to.

You're not agreeing to anything by saying yes. You're simply answering; and answering honestly if you say yes.

Why do you need my permission to make him suffer? Why would you bother at all?

A sigh worked its way into my mind, must've been his.

I have to be summoned. Hired, as it were. I cannot act against a living being of my own volition. I have orders to take him, but it'll be quick and painless. I know what he did to you and I do *want him to suffer. So should you.*

Why should I suffer?

No, I mean you should also want him to suffer.

Oh. Well, I do. But I don't see how—

Together, we can make it happen. It won't be pleasant, however. You'll have to do the heavy lifting…

I thought you were going to do the … doing.

Look, I can't give you all the answers because each new piece of information will simply raise more questions. That's just the nature of the beast. But I can give you a temporary physical form. Together, we'll make him suffer.

What do you get outta this?

I've come for his soul, and I will *be getting it either way. But in the meantime, since you're still here, I figured I'd offer you this chance to get some revenge before I take him.*

Well, I don't really have anything better to do.

Good. One thing you need to understand is that you are energy. Do you know what energy is?

Like when a child is hyper active, they're full of energy?

Something like that. You can think of it that way, if it helps. That energy inside each person transfers to ... outside their bodies after they die. But it doesn't dissipate.

So, there are a bunch of energy balls like me flying around?

No. Typically they either pass through the veil and go to the upper spirit realm, which most of humanity has taken to calling Heaven, or they're forced through the veil and into the lower spirit realm.

Hell.

That's your word for it, yes.

So why am I here? How often does this happen?

You're stuck here because of the events surrounding your death. You feel you've been wronged, and to such an extent that you simply cannot let it go. At the moment of your death, the injustice of it all was like a shot of pure sugar to a toddler's system. Your energy was too strong to pass through the veil, so here you are. And until you're ready, here you'll stay.

What do I have to do to be ready?

I don't have that answer. No one does but you.

So, we make him suffer and then I'll be ready?

I honestly don't know. It may be enough. Or nothing may ever be enough. But if you want to make him pay for what he did to you, for all of it, now's your chance. What's holding you back, Charlotte?

Won't I go to Hell for this? I mean, there's nothin' about hauntings and such in the Bible, that I know of, but I'm pretty sure God won't like it.

You won't make it into the upper spirit realm now. I don't have time to explain it to you. I've either got to take his soul or be re-directed.

Re-directed?

Yes, if you ask me to avenge you, I can hold off on taking his soul until you are satisfied. Whether you do this or not, you're going to the lower spirit realm after you leave this place. It's not as bad as you humans make it out to be. Not for someone like you. You're not malicious.

But isn't ... whatever we might do to him... wouldn't that be considered malicious? Wouldn't I become malicious?

No, you're judged at death based on your actions in life. You weren't that bad. Not bad at all, really. You just weren't particularly good.

Huh. Well that's ... something. So, what are we going to do?

Follow me.

~*~

I could see my hands, vague outlines of them anyway. Through them, past them, a mound of fresh dirt heaped on top of my body a few feet below.

I'm going to transfer just enough of my energy to you so you can manipulate the physical world. You'll have to move quickly because your form cannot hold the excess energy. What you're going to do is use my energy to push the dirt away from your body. Focus on getting the upper half as clear as you can.

All right.

My energy looks like light. Bright white light. Just pretend it's a ball of clay and you should be able to use it.

A ball of clay. Bright white clay. Got it.

Look at your hands, and get ready.

Ready.

My hands glowed, but the light was already fading from my fingertips. Moving fast, I curled my fingers like I was grabbing a plate and pushed them down into the dirt. I shoveled out small piles until the light was gone and my hands dove into the earth without affecting it.

I couldn't see my body yet. Hadn't dug deep enough.

You'll need to go again. Shit.

What's wrong?

I can't give you all of my energy, obviously, and even after your body is somewhat clear, I need to give your corpse some of it.

My… Hold up. What's the plan, exactly?

I *felt* him grinning at me like Hattie Mae used to do when she had a juicy bit of gossip to share.

It's a surprise. You'll like it, though, I'm sure. I'll have to give you more of my energy, there's no avoiding it. Focus on clearing one spot. Really, we just need to see some part of your body, to touch it.

The shudder than ran through me caused some kind of real energy to pass from my hand and into the dirt. The earth just seemed to spread out from under my palm.

Charlotte, what just happened?

You said something about touching my body. Clay used to tell me to touch myself. He liked that. I wouldn't do it, of course. I wasn't gonna make what he did to me any better for him. But he beat the shit out of me every time he asked and I refused. I think it started a whole new thing for him. He knew I'd say no, but he'd ask me anyway just so he could hit me. I think he liked that, too.

I'm so sorry. I didn't mean to make this harder for you. But I think that whatever you were feeling was powerful enough to actually manifest your form in some kind of way.

You mean my feelings can become energy?

I think so. The soul itself, what you are now, is a form of energy. And what is the soul? It's not a physical thing. Hmmm…Try it again.

All right.

I focused on that first night Clay beat me. He was on top of me and he leaned back, pulling my hips up and holding me against him while he sat on his heels.

"Touch yerself."

"What? I…"

"Yer pussy. Rub it."

I shook my head no.

"Don't be a fuckin' prude. Touch your titty or something."

My whole body was shaking. Tears poured down the sides of my face. His wide hand hit me full-on, upside the head.

My ears rang, but everything else stopped. Or seemed to. I couldn't tell. I couldn't even think. My face was still wet and now the left side of it was burning hot. But I couldn't feel the rest of my body. In a way, I was glad. The pain in my face gave me something else to focus on.

But when he hit me again, it brought me back. Whatever relief that brief moment of shock had brought me was gone. I felt everything.

Charlotte…

I heard both the spirit's voice and Clay's snores.

Charlotte, look.

I wasn't at my grave site anymore. I was standing at the foot of Clay's bed. Standing wasn't the right word. I was floating. But my hands were gripping the footboard. I had to pull hard to let go. My fingers had left marks; long indentations framed by splintered wood.

I was energy. Energy wasn't a real thing, but it sure as shit made kids hyper, so it was something. And I made long grooves in the foot board. *I* was something.

And Clay was sleeping.

What should I do to him?

Whatever you want, but you need to direct me. I've got to do something, whether it's aid you or take him.

Can you move things? Like chairs and stuff?

Yes.

Good. I have an idea. First, let's go get my corpse.

~*~

When Clay came to, I—in my rotting carcass—was sitting in the green wingback chair. I'd had my spirit friend turn the chair around so it was facing the bed.

He'd moved the kitchen table to block the door and stacked the four chairs in two pairs, one in front of each window. The only other way out was the small window in the bathroom. Weren't no other windows or rooms in the house, and Clay couldn't fit through the one in the bathroom. He was as trapped as we could get him, for now.

Okay, I've done as you've asked. I need something else to do. What's it gonna be, Charlotte?

Leave him to me. I will summon you when I'm done. Then *you can take him.*

My name is Samael. Call when you are ready.

Thank you, Samael.

~*~

I watched Clay sleeping, wondering what to do. He'd flip his shit when he woke up and saw my rotting body at the foot of his bed—and that'd give me no small amount of satisfaction, no doubt—but then what?

Clay snorted and rolled over onto his side, kicking a leg out from beneath the layers of covers.

I could start there. Yeah, take his covers. That'd get him up, at least.

Getting the corners untucked from the foot of the mattress was the hardest part. From there, one good yank and they slid right off, leaving Clay with no more protection than his flimsy, stained long johns. He rolled onto his back and went to

51

snoring again.

If pulling those covers off was any indication, my body was weaker than the energy that powered it. And it was probably vulnerable to Clay's attacks to boot. I think this'd go better without it.

Oh, I knew then what I'd do. Fighting revulsion and fear, I lay down beside him in his bed then rose from my corpse. That'd fuck him up real good.

I returned to my place at the foot of the bed and practiced. I was stronger without the body, but the trick was in making the connection to something real. Placing my hands on either side of the grooves on the foot board I'd made earlier, I focused on my hands until I could feel the wood in my grip. Then I lifted the bed, just an inch if that, and dropped it.

Clay startled, but went right back to sleep.

So, I did it again. Grip, lift, drop.

He turned over onto his other side, draping an arm across my corpse.

Grip, lift, drop.

That did it. His brows twitched first, his hand patting the odd form and texture beside him where nothing should be. When he finally opened his eyes and inhaled deeply, it was like Christmas morning for me. His scream was the best present I'd ever got.

He tried to shove me off of the bed, but the dead weight didn't move far enough and he couldn't bring himself to touch me again. Instead, he rolled off of his side of the bed and dropped to the floor, scrambling to stand up.

Unable to find his feet, he scooted backward until he hit the green wingback chair now facing his bed. Clay managed to clamber up into the chair, wild-eyed and trembling. He finally tore his gaze away from my corpse, his panicked eyes darting here and there until they landed on me.

I realized then that I had the biggest shit-eating grin on my face. I couldn't help it. This was all just too good. And the best part was, even if he told anyone, they'd never believe him. They'd think he dug up my corpse and put it in his own damn bed! With any luck, they'd hang his sorry ass, too.

I used all my focus, poured all of my hatred and fear, into energy that would breach the veil between the living and the dead so he could hear me when I said, *"No one will believe you."*

It came out as a whisper, but he heard me. Or maybe he read the words my lips formed. Either way, it got through. A low wail tore its way out of his throat as a long shudder wracked his body.

Delighted with the result, I said it again. It didn't matter that he'd turned to run—only to find the way out barred—and probably wouldn't see it or hear it. I just kept repeating the words I'd lived all my miserable life chained by.

"No one will believe you. No one will believe you. No one will believe you."

He managed to get the door clear and head out into the night, screaming for someone, anyone, to help him.

I screamed too, one final time, then contentment and calm washed over me.

Samael, I'm done.

He appeared almost instantly.

Shall I take him now?

Anger hit me at what felt like an injustice, the considerable measure of peace I'd found was gone.

Oh, God. It wasn't enough. It's not fair. If he dies, it's too easy.

You want him to live with this, to suffer with the consequences you've doled out from beyond the grave?

Peace, again, seemed within my grasp.

Yeah, I think I do.

Say the word, Charlotte.

Samael, let Clay live. Let him live a good long while.

As you wish. I'll be moving on now, Charlotte. You're at peace now, but you won't stay that way for long. Not if you remain so near the living. You need to cross the veil into the lower spirit realm.

How do I do that?

Just follow me.

~*~

The Vulture Bus
Daniel Arthur Smith

~*~

Quinn was reading his copy of The Stranger when the call came in. Max flipped the lights on.

"Dammit," said Max. The rig jolted forward.

Quinn finished the page he was reading and then slowly turned to the next. "I told you to take Eighth," he said.

"The app said Tenth is better."

"I told you not to trust the app. Conway took Eighth."

"Conway doesn't have the app. This is faster. See? It's opening up."

Quinn peered over his book to the traffic in front of them. "You know," he said, "there's no reason to beat them."

"I know...It's just efficient."

"Whatever you say."

Max scowled and checked his side mirror. "You think people would put a little more effort into parting the way. I mean, what if the person on the other end was your father, or mother even?"

"Narcissism personified," said Quinn.

"What?"

"Narcissism personified. As in, all they care about is—"

"I know what narcissism is. I meant…why do you have to say something like that?"

"Um. Because it's the truth."

"It's those books you read, all about death."

"I beg to differ. I'd argue that they're all about life."

"How you figure?"

"It's the way a friend of mine saw it." He looked at the cover. "This was her favorite book."

"Odd choice," said Max.

"You had to know her. She was very practical. She once—"

"Here we go," said Max. "They're finally moving."

He slipped the rig into the right lane and twenty-sixth turned into the Elliot-Chelsea Houses, also known as the Chelsea projects. The rescue unit was half a block up.

Conway stood waiting beside his rig. Quinn and Max had been following the same protocol for the last few months to shadow the afternoon calls. Today it meant trailing Conway. That's how it was supposed to work, what they signed up for. The transplant ambulance would turn up at the scene of a death mere minutes after regular paramedics ceased efforts to resuscitate a patient. This time, the call was for a middle-aged female who apparently suffered cardiac arrest.

Max cut the siren and rolled up behind Conway, parting the crowd of curious looky-loos from the curb. Quinn tossed his book on the dash and scanned their riled faces: an assortment of scowls and sneers mixed into blank expression of distrust. The gentrified neighborhood surrounding the Elliot-Chelsea houses may as well have been a million miles away.

The familiar damp odor of the moldy soil in the building's shade wafted over Quinn when he opened his door. He went straight for the gear, not making eye contact with the crowd that had already encircled the back of the rig.

Max opened the rear doors and climbed in.

The closeness of the crowd raised the hairs on his neck.

"There you go," said a man standing a few steps behind him. "If it was a rich person, they would have been saved. But instead, they've sent the Meat Wagon."

"You mean, the Vulture Bus," said another.

Conway joined Quinn at the back.

"Where're we going?" Quinn asked as he took two large cases from Max.

"Twentieth floor," said Conway. "Forty-year-old woman, cardiac arrest—a neighbor called it in. He said she was lucid, but by the time we arrived, she was unresponsive. She's all yours."

"You called it?" asked Quinn.

"Yeah, but I have Hansen giving compressions for you."

"Thanks for that," said Max. He jumped down, swung the doors shut, and then took a case from Quinn. "You coming?" he asked Conway as the three walked to the building.

Conway opened the atrium door and held it for them. "No," he said. "I'll wait down here. The apartment is 20B. You'll see it when you get up there. The guy who called it in said he'd wait for you."

"Is he family?"

Conway shrugged. "I don't know. I don't think so."

Quinn and Max nodded in turn, then made their way through the lobby.

The lobbies of the city's housing authority were all the same: clean but dull, places forgotten in time. The steel paneling in the elevator was the same, wiped countless times with the same custodial rag until all luster had forever abandoned its surface. Even the digital panel–displaying the floors in a series of formed green lights–appeared to be a prisoner of the building.

When the panel hit twenty, the doors slid open.

There were more people standing in the hall than there should have been, neighbors and their friends. An older man, his tight afro white and his eyes glazed, gave the two a quick judging up-down.

"You called it in?"

The man weakly gestured to the left. "This way," he said. Quinn thought the old man may lead the way, but instead he just took a step back to let them pass.

The hall, like the elevator and lobby, was a lifeless corridor, the white paint yellowing from contempt, not age, sunk so deep in despair that the bright light emanating from the dead woman's open apartment door appeared ethereal.

The apartment was reminiscent of so many Quinn had seen. The bright light from the hall was that of the sun shining through the apartment's large bay window. The shelves were lined with assorted memories, odd nick-knacks, a carved ebony menagerie, porcelain figurines, a row of small glass bowls, each a different color—green, blue, orange. A crocheted afghan covered the back of the sofa, the geometric squares within squares design was similar to one Quinn's grandmother owned.

Max's attention drew to the skyline.

"You can see all the way down the Hudson to the statue," he said. "Could you imagine what the price of this place would be? Anywhere else I mean."

"In here," Hansen yelled. "She's in the bedroom."

"All right," said Max.

Sheer white curtains hung in ceiling to floor panels over the bedroom window, calming the light filtering through. Hansen was bent forward, his back to them, shoulders pulsating with the compressions he was giving the body on the bed.

Quinn stepped up beside him and peered at the dead woman. The room fell away from him when he saw her beauty. Her features were soft, the skin smooth, creamy, and radiant.

"Are you ready to take over?" asked Hansen.

"Of course," said Quinn, slipping into Hansen's place. "How long's she been gone."

Hansen shook his arms and hands in the air to wring out his muscles, then flipped his wrist to see his watch. "A good fifteen minutes."

"We should be fine, then."

"Conway told me to keep the blood pumping for you to keep the organs viable."

Quinn, drawn to the face of the sleeping beauty, didn't respond, but Max did. "Yeah. Thanks for that," he said as he opened the first of the two red plastic cases at the foot of the bed.

Hansen leaned over Max' shoulder. "You need help with—"

Quinn cut him off. "We can't administer any drugs until we have permission," he said. "Did you or Conway find anything? An ID? A family member?"

"The door was open when we arrived on scene. Conway thinks a neighbor might have stolen her purse."

"Max," said Quinn.

Max stood and let loose of the plastic bags in his hand. "On it," he said, as he left the room.

"You think she's a donor?" asked Hansen.

"How would I know that?" asked Quinn. "Doesn't matter anyway. This is your first time with us, right?"

"Yep. Been on nights since I started, and you two only roll in the afternoons."

"It works like this. No organs can be removed without getting the family's express consent."

"Even with a donor card? How's that worked out?"

"Not great. Relatives are usually rattled by the site of a transplant team. Some have a religious objection to organ donation in general and get pissed when they find out uncle Eddie's been injected with fluids. For other families, it's political."

"Political?"

"Rightly or wrongly," Quinn glanced up at Hansen, "they question whether the paramedics curtailed their lifesaving efforts because a patient had valuable organs."

"I never thought of that."

"Now you know. Maybe you can go downstairs and ask around. I'd rather not keep this up if we don't need to." He nodded toward the woman.

"Yeah. Sure," Hansen said on his way out.

Quinn kept up compressions for another thirty seconds, until he was alone with the body, then he stopped.

He placed the back of his hand against her cheek, still warm—so familiar.

He slid his hand to the nape of her neck, and gently raised her head.

"Come on," he said softly. And, as if lured by his call, a golden light crept from where he held her behind her head and continued to brighten until the room was aglow.

Her lips, deliciously full, curved up into a smile and her blue eyes opened.

~*~

Quinn continued to hold the woman who, a moment before, had been dead. With his other hand, he took hers into his own.

She did not acknowledge him at first. Rather, she stared toward the ceiling. When it appeared that the last of her dream had faded, she shifted her attention to him.

"What happened?" she asked, her voice velvet, her accent exotic. "Who are you?"

"I was going to ask you the same thing," said Quinn. "What do you remember?"

"A boy. He followed me into my apartment and grabbed my bag. I called for help and he struck me, then he fled. The last I remember, Mister Johnson was trying to wake me."

"Mister Johnson. Yeah. He called us."

"But who are you?"

"I'm a paramedic, of sorts."

Her eyes dropped to the snake and rod embroidered on the patch on his sleeve. "Yes," she said. "But how'd you know?"

"That you weren't human?"

Her eyes narrowed.

"You really don't recognize me?" he asked. "Look harder…beyond this body."

She said nothing at first. Then, "Can it be? Quinn? Is it really you?"

"Yes, Cassandra," said Quinn. "My love, It's me." He squeezed her hand tighter and brought it to his chest. "I can't believe I've found you after so long. When they sent you to this quadrant, I feared I'd never see you again."

"Is that why you're here?" she asked. "Have you been sent by the syndicate?"

"Yes. But not the one who sent you."

"What do you mean?"

"So much has changed since you left. When the value of this time period was reported back, the syndicates began a bidding war. It became a massive power struggle that turned bloody. Your syndicate suffered most. They lost their charter."

"I don't understand. I'm still getting reports to continue my work. How could that be?"

"I don't know for sure. But there is a faction that's held out, they're trying to sway the council. They've kept operatives in this time, to build strength."

"That explains a lot," she said.

"How so?"

"The nature of my missions has changed. More sabotage and acquisition than eco stability. I didn't question it. I should have, but I wanted to earn my way back to you."

"You," he hesitated. "You couldn't have."

"What do you mean?"

"The syndicate that has the charter on the city. They have a standing order to eliminate any members of the faction."

"Is that what you do? What you've become? An assassin?"

"Not at all. I was sent here to save lives—save the dead anyway. I identify bodies for relocation."

Cassandra rose to embrace him. "That's wonderful," she said. "You and I can be together again." She pressed her body against his. "I can't believe it. It's been so long."

Quinn pulled her into him and rested his chin on her head.

"There's so much I have to tell you," she said. Her voice told him that she had begun to weep. "Things I want to show you. There are things in this time you wouldn't believe— treasures hidden away. The people that live here have no idea. Have you been to the north? To see the snow?"

"No," was all Quinn said.

"It's amazing. It never melts. I must take you there. And the whales—have you seen the whales?"

Again, a simple, "No."

Cassandra pulled her head away. "Something's

wrong…What is it?"

"The mission has changed. You said you figured it out."

"What does that matter? We can be together now."

"You don't understand. You can't leave here. Your body has already been tagged as a vessel. To change that would draw an investigation. Either way…"

"Either way? Either way what?"

"You'll have to be…"

"I see." She rose from the bed and went over to the window. She pulled the curtain to the side to see the world unfiltered. "It makes sense. I can't appear to have miraculously came back to life." She spun to face him. "Terminate this body."

Quinn shook his head. "I can't do that."

"You must. Or they'll kill us both."

"That would be tantamount to killing you."

Cassandra went to Quinn. She reached her hands to his face and held his cheeks. She pressed her lips against his and then pulled away. "If you love me you'll do this."

"I only now found you."

"You've never lost me. Our love transcends these bodies. It transcends time."

Cassandra lay back down on the bed, in the same position she had been in when he arrived. "You have to," she said. "I insist."

"I don't want to," he said. "We can go now. The two of us. We'll sneak out the side of the building. We'll take a bus. We can pay cash. We'll go up the Hudson, out of the city, past the small towns, across the country, to the mountains. I've heard there are others, from your faction, that have hidden away. We can do the same."

"You know we can't. They'll find us."

Quinn held his gaze. "My greatest regret was letting you leave before me. I'm not going to make that mistake again."

"You have to…Please."

Again, he was lost in her. He had loved her so—loved her so. An ache filled his vessel, his body. A pain he shouldn't have been able to feel. They were beings of spirit, not form, their bodies mere vessels, their hearts did not beat. And then it came to him.

"I have an answer. A way we might be together."

"I don't understand."

"Join me in this vessel. We can be together forever."

Quinn bent forward to kiss Cassandra one last time.

~*~

The moldy odor from beside the sidewalk wafted up to Quinn as he stepped out of the building. Except he was no longer Quinn. The crowd was still gathered, some new faces taking the place of others. "Ya'll are butchers," decreed an old woman.

"Vultures," said a younger voice.

Quinn who was no longer Quinn, climbed into the rig without making eye contact. "Did you call us in available?" he asked.

"Right after I called the medical examiner," said Max. "They'll be here to take her to the morgue soon enough. A shame, really. I'm sure she was viable. She was a beauty."

"Yes," Quinn smiled. "She was." He picked up the paperback from the dash, looked at the cover, and opened it to page one. "This is my favorite. Narcissism personified."

~*~

ABOUT THE AUTHORS

J.N. Lavelle is an author and photographer from West Michigan. When he's not spending time with his beautiful wife and four children, he's probably at the dog park with his three pugs, Dragon, Dylan and Mr. Sparkles and his annoying dachshund, Lady. After he's done playing with the pugs and tucking the kids into bed, he explores the paranormal world through his writing.

For more information, visit
darkhorsestudios3.wixsite.com/lavelle

P.K. Tyler is the author of Speculative Fiction and other Genre Bending novels. She's also published works as Pavarti K. Tyler and had projects appear on the **USA TODAY** Bestseller's List.

Pav attended Smith College and graduated with a degree in Theatre. She lived in New York, where she worked as a Dramaturge, Assistant Director and Production Manager on productions both on and off-Broadway. Later, Pavarti went to work in the finance industry for several international law firms.

Now located in Baltimore Maryland, she lives with her husband, two daughters and two terrible dogs. When not penning science fiction books and other speculative fiction novels, she twists her mind by writing horror and erotica.

For more information, visit
pktyler.com

Jessica West (a.k.a. West1Jess) is currently pursuing a state of self-induced psychosis, also known as writing. In the past, she has worked for Wal-Mart, a lawyer, and a bank. Now if she could just get a couple years experience with the IRS and the NSA, world domination is in the bag.

Jess lives in Acadiana with three daughters still young enough to think she's cool and a husband who knows better but likes her anyway.

For more information, visit
west1jess.com

Daniel Arthur Smith is the author of the international bestsellers *Hugh Howey Lives*, *The Cathari Treasure*, *The Somali Deception*, and a few other novels and short stories. He also curates the phenomenal short fiction series *Tales from the Canyons of the Damned*.

He was raised in Michigan and graduated from Western Michigan University where he studied philosophy, with focus on cognitive science, meta-physics, and comparative religion. He began his career as a bartender, barista, poetry house proprietor, teacher, and then became a technologist and futurist for the Fortune 100 across the Americas and Europe.

Daniel has traveled to over 300 cities in 22 countries, residing in Los Angeles, Kalamazoo, Prague, Crete, and now writes in Manhattan where he lives with his wife and young sons.

For more information, visit danielarthursmith.com

~*~

www.ingramcontent.com/pod-product-compliance
Lightning Source LLC
Chambersburg PA
CBHW020315150626
46552CB00022B/2894